NOTHING TO THIS

ONE WILD NIGHT

SCARLETT FINN

Also by Scarlett Finn

GO NOVELS
GO WITH IT
GO IT ALONE
GO ALL OUT
GO ALL IN
GO FULL CIRCLE

EXILE
HIDE & SEEK
KISS CHASE

WRECK & RUIN
RUIN ME
RUIN HIM

THE BRANDED SERIES
BRANDED
SCARRED
MARKED

FORBIDDEN PREQUEL DUET
ALL. ONLY.
ONLY YOURS

THE FORBIDDEN NOVELS
FORBIDDEN DESIRE
FORBIDDEN WANT
FORBIDDEN WISH
FORBIDDEN NEED
FORBIDDEN BOND

BOMBSHELLS & BILLIONAIRES (ROXIVERSE)
NOTHING TO HIDE
NOTHING TO LOSE
NOTHING IN BETWEEN: ONE
NOTHING TO DECLARE
NOTHING TO US
NOTHING IN BETWEEN: TWO
NOTHING TO SAY
NOTHING TO GAIN
NOTHING IN BETWEEN: THREE
NOTHING TO YOU
NOTHING TO THIS PREQUEL: ONE WILD NIGHT
NOTHING TO THIS
NOTHING IN BETWEEN: FOUR
NOTHING TO DO
NOTHING TO NO ONE
NOTHING TO FEAR
NOTHING TO DENY
NOTHING TO BEAT
NOTHING TO THE WEDDING
NOTHING TO TELL
NOTHING TO IT
NOTHING TO SEE
NOTHING TO WIN
NOTHING TO OFFER
NOTHING TO PROVE

LOVE AGAINST THE ODDS STANDALONE COLLECTION
SWEET SEAS
HEIR'S AFFAIR
RESCUED
MAESTRO'S MUSE
GETTING TRICKY
THIRTEEN
REMEMBER WHEN...
RELUCTANT SUSPICION
XY FACTOR

KINDRED SERIES
RAVEN
SWALLOW
CUCKOO
SWIFT
FALCON
FINCH

MISTAKE DUET
MISTAKE ME NOT
SLEIGHT MISTAKE

LOST & FOUND
LOST
FOUND

THE EXPLICIT SERIES
EXPLICIT INSTRUCTION
EXPLICIT DETAIL
EXPLICIT MEMORY

TO DIE FOR...
TO DIE FOR TRUTH
TO DIE FOR HONOR
TO DIE FOR VIRTUE
TO DIE FOR DUTY
TO DIE FOR LOVE

RISQUÉ & HARROW INTERTWINED
TAKE A RISK
FIGHTING FATE
RISK IT ALL
FIGHTING BACK
GAME OF RISK

ACTION

ONE

ALMOST SIX YEARS AGO

HOW DID THIS HAPPEN?

God, his kiss was… powerful. Confident. Demanding. Shit, whatever consumed him infected her too. Their disease was pure lust and neither of them fought it. Let it take them down.

Her back hit the elevator wall. Roaming hands fought fabric, searching, squeezing, stroking.

"Fuck, I want you," he breathed.

"More."

Temptation stole his mouth to her throat, her breast, her cleavage. Damnit, her body tingled, her skin fizzed. This guy was everywhere; somehow in every part of her. And completely in control. Plucking her up, he twined her legs around him, letting his mouth return to the kiss it'd denied hers.

Shit.

They'd been drinking.

Hooking up wasn't smart.

Strangers. In a hotel. Anonymous.

So many things were wrong with the picture.

Red flags flew everywhere.

But… what the hell? Inhaling his kiss, she gave herself to it, pushing his tongue with hers, matching his furious need. Fuck, his body was solid. She was too high up. Couldn't feel—

He dropped her back to her feet and grabbed her hand to rush them from the elevator into a room. A very private, dark—living room. They didn't stop, no. This was heading somewhere far more horizontal. He hurried through a door in the corner and swung her into his arms, squeezing her body to his.

"Last chance to back out."

She actually laughed. "You think I'm here against my will?" Sliding her hands up his chest, she pushed his jacket off and got to work unfastening his shirt buttons.

He ducked, tracing his lips across hers, then his head fell back. "Even your voice is hot. Damnit, you're a siren I can't resist."

Snagging his jaw with the gentle press of her fingernails, she tempted it down again. "Looks to me like you're resisting," she murmured. "You want to slow down?"

With a crooked brow, he walked, backing her toward the bed. "In a rush, Siren?"

"You got me going, now you're hitting the brakes. Pussy tease."

Jolting her body from his, he ripped open her shirt and tossed her onto the bed.

"No brakes," he said, casting off his button down and shoes.

Shit, that physique. Solid was right. Defined, delicious, way more than the clumsy jocks she'd been with in college. Definition like that wasn't bulk, it was finesse. Perfect.

Her fingers couldn't keep away as he descended above her. Their mouths met slowly. A gentle press, a delicate touch.

"Now, JD," she whispered, arching up, encouraging his mouth's exploration of her neck.

Hard. Mm. And just right. His cock, encased in fabric, teased her. More. She wanted more.

Their kiss masked the shedding of her clothes. Skin on skin wasn't enough. Coiling her legs higher around him, she loosened his belt to liberate her prize.

"We can go slow, baby."

"No, we fucking can't," she gasped, squeezing him tight. "Your cock agrees with me. You're outvoted."

A gruff laugh preceded his kiss. The way his hips moved with her fist could be involuntary, but the motion betrayed him. He wanted it. Wanted her. And she wanted him to fulfill his desire. In her. All night long.

"Good." The edge of need in his voice suggested his restraint was slipping. "I'm not in the mood to take my time."

"That a promise?"

As satisfaction relaxed her, he plunged into her. Shit, now who was the one wearing that satisfaction?

Her teeth dug into her lip as he moved slow, his eyes locked on hers. Warming her up, easing her in, whatever it was, experiencing him like that gave her something new, something unexpected. A gratification that touched every part of her, inside and out. A belonging that felt safe, even while alarm bells rang.

Tightening the circle of her legs, she pulled him deeper, angling her hips, enhancing their connection.

"More." The word du jour. "Harder. Fuck me, JD."

Her day hadn't started with promise. Her evening hadn't begun with him. No, this guy wandered into her path from nowhere. The unexpected was exciting, an adventure. Sometimes life just happened and all you could do was enjoy the ride. And a ride like him didn't come along every day.

Trust her to go to bed with a stubborn, egotistical agitator.

How did this happen?

TWO

EARLIER THAT NIGHT

OH, HER FEET HURT. Most every woman on the continent would know exactly the pinch and squeeze that abraded her skin. Heels. Why had she thought they were a good idea for her first tech expo? What was she trying to prove? And, given she traveled alone, who was she proving it to?

It was early, as the almost deserted hotel bar highlighted, but still evening, giving her the green light for alcohol. After five p.m. was the rule everywhere, right? She slid onto the central stool at the long bar and breathed out her bliss when the pressure left her feet. Yeah, they still ached, but she'd take any win.

The bartender came wandering over. "What can I get you?"

"Rum and Coke… and a tequila shot."

"Bad day?"

"Long day," she said on a smile as he went to fill her order.

Maybe she should eat. Did she want to eat? When was the last time she ate? Her breakfast coffee was a distant memory.

"Excuse me."

The masculine voice brought her attention around. Mm, hello. Tall, gorgeous, shirt, tie. Serious. Playing with him might be fun. If only she wasn't so damned exhausted.

"Can I help you?" she asked because he just stood there glaring. If this was a move, the guy wasn't too smooth. "Is something wrong?"

"That's my seat."

Glancing along the bar, she twisted to check out the line of empty stools behind her. "Seriously? It's not like there's nowhere to sit. How is this your seat?"

He nodded to something beyond her. "That's my drink."

She looked over her shoulder at the all-but-empty whiskey glass. "It's closer to the other stool." It was a judgement call, was it closer? Yes, by a hair. "And it's all the way across at the bartender's side. That suggests finished to me."

Her smile narrowed his eyes. "You're not going to move?"

"I'm not going to move."

On principle? Partly. She also didn't want to put weight on her poor feet again.

"Okay."

That was that then. Bye, guy.

The bartender came over to put down her drinks. "If my feet didn't hurt so much, I'd jump up on this bar and kiss you."

"Put it on my tab, Mike. I need another," said a male voice behind her.

On a snicker, the bartender went away and there was the seat guy, sliding onto the stool next to hers.

"Are you kidding me? There are fifty seats in this room. You're picking that one?"

"I could say the same to you," he said. "Of all the places you could've picked, you chose mine."

"It wasn't yours," she said on a sneer. "You don't own the stool."

"Know the guy who owns the hotel."

"Oh, and I'm just so impressed," she feigned wonder with a hearty dose of sarcasm. "Maybe you should ask him to put a plaque on it. Post security to protect it when you go to the men's room."

"Maybe I will."

"Won't save you tonight. This is my seat. And I'm not going anywhere," she said, tossing the tequila shot down her throat. "For a very long time." Mike came over with the seat guy's drink. "Now I need another one of these." She raised her shot glass. "Two. If Mr. Connected over here is paying."

As Mike retreated, a hand appeared in front of her. "Jamison." Oh, Mr. Connected. "Dawes."

"Good for you." She landed a suspicious eye on him. "You married?"

"No." His hand just stayed there. "You?"

"No. Why would you ask me that?"

Except, her head tilted, hadn't she just…?

"You asked me."

"To find out if you're a sleazy bar creeper who picks up women in bars while your wife waits at home."

"And you couldn't be a sleazy bar creeper who picks up men in bars while your husband waits at home?"

Touché. Intriguing.

"Rylee," she said and shook her head. "But I don't want to shake your hand."

"Because…?"

"I don't know where it's been."

That wasn't exactly the truth. Tequila was

swirling in her stomach and his eyes had darkened. Oh, shit. This wasn't the time to make bad decisions. If she could feel his pull just sitting next to him, touching wasn't going to ease the burden. No, damn, and now she wanted to touch so much more than just his hand. She should've eaten something.

"I took a call," he said, his palm settling on the bar. "Didn't use the restroom." She wasn't even thinking that. He raised his glass. "Should we toast?"

"To what? I'm sitting here alone and didn't invite you to join me."

"I could argue you joined me," he said, sipping his liquor. "You put yourself in my path."

What was fate up to? The guy wasn't wrong. And her snippy, cynical woman bit wasn't doing its job. He was supposed to be deterred, not encouraged.

She sighed. "You were at the tech expo, Jamison Dawes?" Everyone around was. He nodded, confirming that notion. "It's amazing, isn't it? So much talent concentrated in a space that's… Think if the building went on fire, humanity would be set back ten years? Technologically?"

"Twenty, at least," he said. "Thinking about arson?"

"I'm thinking about how much we rely on technology and how it's taken over our lives. We don't even talk to each other anymore. No one just bumps into someone and hits it off. It's contrived. Online. The web or apps. There's an app for literally everything. And we can't trust anyone in the digital world. Not even ourselves."

"We bumped into each other."

"Hmm," she said, relaxing.

The precise haircut. The blue of his eyes. This was a guy who didn't need to go online for any kind of relief. If he was interested in a woman, just looking at her would be enough. And then he dealt the killer blow and smiled.

"You're staring," he said on a whisper of a laugh. "You don't think we'll hit it off?"

Maybe. Bad idea. Yet, for some reason, she didn't shut him down. "The night is young. I guess we'll have to see how this plays out."

"I guess we will."

And when she raised her glass, he was nice enough to touch his to it. The tequila shooters were there when she put down her rum. Picking one up, she handed the other to him.

"To bumping into each other," she said.

"To hitting it off."

They both drank. And he was confident. Mm, she pushed her hips a little deeper into the stool.

"Why'd you leave the expo?"

"Saw what I came to see," he said. "Why did you leave?"

"I've been there since first thing this morning. I was taking more of a macro view… I got all the macro I needed."

"What's your field?"

"Branding," she said and shrugged. "I've been with my company for almost a year. They always send the recent graduates to things like this at least once. And it's research. I have to know what our competitors are doing to know how to beat it."

"Ah, you were spying."

She laughed. "I suppose you could call it that."

"Learn anything interesting?"

"Maybe. What about you? Are you a tech genius pedaling your wares?"

"No. That's a definite no." He drank, his eyes staying on hers, dancing with a mischief that drew her closer. "I'm building my business."

"And you're looking for inspiration?"

"You could say that."

"There's something so uncivilized about the order of these things," she said, sliding her glass closer to his as her body turned his way. "Chaos with a floor plan and fire exits."

"Isn't that just an analogy of life?"

"It's all chaos?"

"You must be familiar with chaos theory."

A burst of laughter accompanied her smile. "Theoretical physics? Wow, that's a unique pickup angle. You must be confident."

"It's just mathematics," he drawled, all swagger. "And I didn't know I was trying to pick you up."

"Yes, you did." Her crossed legs bumped his. "You wanted to pick me up the second you saw me in your seat."

"Yeah, to dump you somewhere else."

There was a warmth in those eyes, an ease of confidence, that offered comfort. More than just alight, the flicker of heat tantalized her aroused curiosity.

"You could've said nothing," she murmured, leaning in. "Accepted my disrespect and moved on. You didn't."

"I'm not the kind of guy who moves on that easy."

"Get attached to things, do you?"

"Let's just say I'm not easily dissuaded."

"And I'm no pushover."

"I can tell. Do you drive your boss nuts? If you're new, maybe you haven't been there long enough to piss the guy off."

"My supervisor is a woman," she said, lifting her glass. "And I've been with the company for a year, so she must like something about me."

"Not if she sent you here." His eyes narrowed.

"You must be fresh out of college. You graduate this year?"

"Wrong again. I finished college last year."

"So you got this job out of college?"

"I started as an intern."

And damn, he enjoyed being right. That beaming smile was evidence enough. "You're just a baby."

"I turned twenty-three three months ago. I am not a baby."

"Ah, in the grand scheme of things you are, baby," he said, laying a forearm on the bar as he tipped more liquor into his mouth.

Sliding to the edge of her stool, she bowed until her lips were just a whisper from his ear. "Thought men liked younger women."

When his head turned, their lips got so close, she could taste the bitterness of his drink on his breath. "Got a daddy fetish?"

"Do I?" she asked, laughing as she sat up straight again. "No, I don't have a daddy fetish."

"Shame, I like a woman who does what she's told."

"Sorry, I've always been a rebel."

"Saying that, I don't mind a bad girl."

She laughed. "Make up your mind."

"Variety keeps life interesting."

"Yeah, life's a rollercoaster." She sighed and rested an elbow on the bar. "Is this as good as it gets?"

"Life? I don't know, we're all on the same road. Just passing through. It's what we make it. And I'm shocked, tech expos aren't your idea of a good time?"

"If they are for you, then you have big problems, buddy."

"What made you choose branding?"

"It chose me," she said, her fingers curling under her jaw to support her head. "Sort of." She inhaled. "I had to pick a major and coloring in wasn't an option."

He laughed. "Coloring in?"

"I'm an artist," she said. "God, that sounds pretentious. Since I was young, sketching, drawing, painting—it's what I love."

"Not a lot of money in that."

"No, there is not," she agreed, stroking the rim of her glass. "In marketing, I spend a lot of time manifesting other peoples' ideas, but it's work, you know? And it pays the rent."

"Ultimately?" he asked. "What's your goal?" She frowned. "Where do you see yourself in five years? Ten years?"

"Global domination isn't on the agenda. I just want my own slice of the world. My own little corner. Somewhere safe and happy, somewhere I can pursue my dreams. Even if I'm only moonlighting."

"You're practical. Pragmatic. Unusual for someone your age. Where did all the naïve idealism go? You're fresh-faced. Where's the wonder?"

"I like to think I'm smarter than that. My mom died just before I graduated high school. I got a scholarship and lived off her insurance money for a while. Worked so many jobs I lost count."

"Waitressing?"

"Sometimes. I preferred doing clerical stuff. Filing. Typing. Answering phones. I did assistant work, picked up training courses where I could to make my résumé more appealing. When you're alone in the world, you grow up fast. There's no one around to prop me up. You've got to hold your head up and charge on. Overcome obstacles, don't surrender to them."

"Wow, that's harsh."

"You think I'm wrong?"

"No, I think you just got hotter."

As his smile rose, she let herself respond in kind.

"See, I knew you were trying to pick me up."

"Of course I'm trying to pick you up," he said and gave the bartender a signal for more drinks. "How am I doing so far?"

"It's getting better by the minute."

THREE

"I DON'T THINK THERE'S SPACE."

"To dance?" she asked, laughing at him as she turned to scan the room. Except, huh, he was right. How had she missed the growing crowd? "Oh… It got busy."

People swarmed around tables and in corners. Judging by the getup, they'd been at the convention center too. As more flocked in, the space dwindled. It would only get worse as the night progressed.

"The expo must've let out."

And she hadn't even noticed. The noise level was high and, come to think of it, their own volume had gone up too. Getting closer was no hardship. His cologne was intoxicating. Had her mind been so befuddled that her surroundings became a blur? Yes.

"How rude," she said, meeting his eye again.

The bar's atmosphere had gone from intimate to raucous. That didn't suit their conversation at all. What a shame. Things were getting interesting; she wasn't ready to say goodnight.

"We could get them thrown out."

Trust him to have a crazy plan. "All of them?" she asked on a snicker. "How would we do that?"

"I have my ways."

The man of mystery thing didn't really fit with logic. "Wouldn't it make more sense for us to go somewhere else?"

"At this time of night around here, everywhere will be busy."

Good point. All hotels and venues around town would hold events, in whatever form, to entertain the influx. Privacy wouldn't be easy to find.

"It was nice while it lasted, but I'm not in the mood for crowds," she said, draining her glass. "I had a good time." Something she hadn't expected when she first sat down. "You're an interesting guy, Jamison Dawes."

"My suite has a bar."

Their eyes met. Oh, fuck, don't make bad decisions, Rylee. She was kidding herself. The entire night had been heading this way from the second he joined her. Was it too brazen to just agree? Should she play hard to get? Resisting would be better for decorum, for her reputation.

Except if he accepted her polite reluctance, the night would be over. She couldn't say no when she really meant yes. Then she'd only kick herself later. Screw decorum.

Sweeping up her purse, she hopped off the stool. "Lead the way."

While he paid their tab, she looped her purse strap over her shoulder. Throwing caution to the wind wasn't always a bad idea. There was something to being anonymous, separate from their real lives, it was an adventure. And who knew when she'd get some back at home? Talent at work was on the sparse side. Spotlight Solutions was not a hotbed of passion. She hadn't seen a single male model on their payroll. This guy? Oh, he could definitely occupy space in glossy magazines meant to torment and tease women.

"You okay?"

Her mind had been wandering, but his voice brought it back. She gestured out, and with a hand on her lower back, he steered them to the elevator. It was a drink. He'd said "bar" not "bed." Maybe sex wasn't on his mind. Perhaps she was just scintillating conversation.

Hardly. If conversation was what he wanted, plenty of wiser minds had just poured out of the convention center. People like that, men and women alike, could be inexhaustible when it came to discussing their passions. Especially when surrounded by other like minds.

The doors opened, and they stepped inside. All night their eyes had teased and played as their lips taunted and aroused. Now they couldn't even look at each other. Standing side by side, almost like strangers, the tension grew as the doors closed, shutting them inside.

Was he regretting the offer? Did he lie about being married? Maybe the cues were all wrong. Since when had she been able to read male minds? Never, that's when. Her hand swayed from her side, just a little, but it was enough. The second her finger brushed his, he turned to scoop his hands around her head, and their mouths clashed.

Instinct took over. Her head spun, making sense of nothing while understanding her purpose. Her only purpose. That kiss. Lights sparkled behind her eyelids as her arms twined around his neck.

How did this happen?

God, his kiss was… powerful. Confident. Demanding. Shit, whatever consumed him infected her too. Their disease was pure lust and neither of them fought it. Let it take them down.

Her back hit the elevator wall. Roaming hands fought fabric, searching, squeezing, stroking.

"Fuck, I want you," he breathed.

"More."

Temptation stole his mouth to her throat, her breast, her cleavage. Damnit, her body tingled, her skin fizzed. This guy was everywhere; somehow in every part of her. And completely in control. Plucking her up, he twined her legs around him, letting his mouth return to the kiss it'd denied hers.

Shit.

They'd been drinking.

Hooking up wasn't smart.

Strangers. In a hotel. Anonymous.

So many things were wrong with the picture.

Red flags flew everywhere.

But… what the hell? Inhaling his kiss, she gave herself to it, pushing his tongue with hers, matching his furious need. Fuck, his body was solid. She was too high up. Couldn't feel—

He dropped her back to her feet and grabbed her hand to rush them from the elevator into a room. A very private, dark—living room. They didn't stop, no. This was heading somewhere far more horizontal. He hurried through a door in the corner and swung her into his arms, squeezing her body to his.

"Last chance to back out."

She actually laughed. "You think I'm here against my will?" Sliding her hands up his chest, she pushed his jacket off and got to work unfastening his shirt buttons.

He ducked, tracing his lips across hers, then his head fell back. "Even your voice is hot. Damnit, you're a siren I can't resist."

Snagging his jaw with the gentle press of her fingernails, she tempted it down again. "Looks to me like you're resisting," she murmured. "You want to slow down?"

With a crooked brow, he walked, backing her toward the bed. "In a rush, Siren?"

"You got me going, now you're hitting the brakes. Pussy tease."

Jolting her body from his, he ripped open her shirt and tossed her onto the bed.

"No brakes," he said, casting off his button down and shoes.

Shit, that physique. Solid was right. Defined, delicious, way more than the clumsy jocks she'd been with in college. Definition like that wasn't bulk, it was finesse. Perfect.

Her fingers couldn't keep away as he descended above her. Their mouths met slowly. A gentle press, a delicate touch.

"Now, JD," she whispered, arching up, encouraging his mouth's exploration of her neck.

Hard. Mm. And just right. His cock, encased in fabric, teased her. More. She wanted more.

Their kiss masked the shedding of her clothes. Skin on skin wasn't enough. Coiling her legs higher around him, she loosened his belt to liberate her prize.

"We can go slow, baby."

"No, we fucking can't," she gasped, squeezing him tight. "Your cock agrees with me. You're outvoted."

A gruff laugh preceded his kiss. The way his hips moved with her fist could be involuntary, but the motion betrayed him. He wanted it. Wanted her. And she wanted him to fulfill his desire. In her. All night long.

"Good." The edge of need in his voice suggested his restraint was slipping. "I'm not in the mood to take my time."

"That a promise?"

As satisfaction relaxed her, he plunged into her.

Shit, now who was the one wearing that satisfaction?

Her teeth dug into her lip as he moved slow, his eyes locked on hers. Warming her up, easing her in, whatever it was, experiencing him like that gave her something new, something unexpected. A gratification that touched every part of her, inside and out. A belonging that felt safe, even while alarm bells rang.

Tightening the circle of her legs, she pulled him deeper, angling her hips, enhancing their connection.

"More." The word du jour. "Harder. Fuck me, JD."

Her day hadn't started with promise. Her evening hadn't begun with him. No, this guy wandered into her path from nowhere. The unexpected was exciting, an adventure. Sometimes life just happened and all you could do was enjoy the ride. And a ride like him didn't come along every day.

Trust her to go to bed with a stubborn, egotistical agitator.

How did this happen?

His speed grew in time with his obvious need. Wasn't so funny to tease anymore. Panting breaths and moving bodies took the place of words. Her hands kept wandering, learning his lines and sinking down to feel the point of their connection. He didn't slow or stop. Their eyes met when she circled him with a forefinger and thumb, squeezing the root of him every time it plundered deep.

"JD," she found her words and her fingers loosened above her clit. "Shit, JD."

Because she was there, right there. Whining in pleasure, her body became more about her own climax than anything his was doing.

"Good girl," he murmured.

Oh, fuck. The pressure eclipsed her ability to hear or see or breathe. Lost in that rigid moment, she wanted to live there, right there in that delight forever.

FOUR

HE LANDED ON HIS BACK next to her.

Shit.

That had been…

Her blurred vision hadn't recovered its focus. "Damn, I was easy."

He kissed her shoulder and her ear, scooping an arm around her. "Some things are inevitable."

"I didn't even know I needed that, but shit, I needed that. Do you do this a lot?"

"Pick up women in bars?" he asked. "No… Now that you mention it, I haven't done it in a long time."

"No takers?"

"I just got out of a relationship."

So she was a rebound. Good. At least there was no expectation. How long had it been since she'd got laid? Months. Work was becoming her life. Routine and focus were her friends, and relationships rarely offered either.

"Was it true love?"

"Gabby? No. Maybe we thought so. Isn't

everything love until it's not?"

"Anything that lasts more than a week, I guess. Why are we so bad at it?" she asked rhetorically. "Humans. In general. We're so bad at this."

"Not bad at this part," he said, trailing his fingers up her body.

"Sex? No, we're not. Is that why relationships are hard, because sex is so easy? Any of us could just fall into bed with anyone. Fluid exchange is simple, but when it comes to putting our thoughts and feelings into words… Language is where it gets difficult. Especially when we don't know what our opposite is thinking and feeling."

"It's not easy. Picking someone to spend our lives with. We want to get it right."

"It feels like pressure. Relationships come with expectation. We don't want to offend or upset our partner, usually we have to face them again the next day. Or we share a circle of friends and everyone wants to get involved. Sometimes it's easier to relax with strangers. We can be more of our honest self without worrying about fallout."

"I don't think we can call ourselves strangers anymore," he said, kissing her hair. At what point did someone become a friend? Somewhere between kissing and orgasm maybe. "Do you want something to eat?"

After another kiss, he sat up to snag something from the nightstand and put it in her hands: a room service menu.

"You said something about a bar up here," she said, laying the menu on his legs when he propped himself against the headboard. "Where's that at?"

"We should eat something. Soak up some of the alcohol."

"You worried?" she asked, flipping over to crawl to the head of the bed. "Think you took advantage of me?"

"I think you need your energy," he said, perusing the menu. "That was just the opening act. The main event is still to come."

"Yes," she said, pushing the menu aside to slide into his lap, straddling him. "There better be more to come."

His kiss spoke to her. The gentle touch of their lips, the angling here to there, the way they sensed each other's needs and anticipated their actions was poetry. If the alcohol was responsible for their innate movements, she'd become an alcoholic trying to recapture the high.

As her hands landed on his shoulders, his fingers tunneled into her hair. They needed to touch, to be closer, to be more than just two people. Rising, she took him into her body again. God knew how long they'd been kissing. Time was irrelevant. Everything was irrelevant except the hard length of him occupying her.

"JD," she whispered, her eyes closing.

But he kept her head, catching its weight when it tried to drop back. "Stay with me," he murmured, slow and sure, like an order she couldn't ignore. "Open your eyes."

Her eyelids parted, though not much. Somehow, the visual contact heightened the pressure building within her. Moving faster, she grabbed for him, and he caught her hips, steadying her, moving with her to join her over the finish line.

"Oh, it's so not fair," she said, relaxing her whole body on his.

Her bones became rubber, malleable, incapable of holding her together. It didn't matter that he was still inside her or that her skin was clammy from the exertion. All she wanted to do was stay right there.

"Not fair?" Stroking a hand down her hair, he scratched her scalp. "What isn't fair?"

"That I'll never find an orgasm like that again."

It still tingled through her, quaking her thighs, shimmering within her sensitive pussy in small joyous jolting aftershocks. Like every time her body recalled the pleasure, a shimmer of memory teased her to arousal again.

"It's not gone anywhere yet. Hungry?"

"We should carb up," she said, scratching his bicep.

"Get ready for a marathon?"

She laughed. "It could be a long night, lover."

***

THEY ORDERED FOOD and got more drinks. She didn't even care about the time. It was tomorrow already, she knew that, but it didn't matter. In the cocoon of their intimacy, they were invincible, and the night was still young.

"You didn't tell me about your business," she said, accepting the drink he handed over before joining her on the bed again. "Do you make anything?"

"Money," he said, offering a toast. "Tonight forever."

She didn't know what that meant exactly but touched her glass to his anyway. "Money? A lot of money?"

"Enough."

Taking in their environment, her curiosity grew. "Is your company paying for this? The big fancy suite?" Not that she could claim to know anything about it beyond the bedroom and bathroom. "This can't be cheap."

"It's company expenses. Start as you mean to go on."

"You're just starting?"

"God, no, and I wouldn't go back to the start

either. Stakes get higher in line with profits. Risks are more of a gamble when you're responsible for people's lives."

"Your employees?"

He nodded behind his glass. "As we accrue assets, our employee numbers increase."

She tilted her head. "Why do I feel like you get off on that?"

With a laugh, he put his glass on the nightstand. "Because you're perceptive." When she finished her mouthful, he took her glass to put it by his. "It's an adrenaline high. And it's not about the people as individuals, there's a thrill to knowing good deals guarantee jobs. It's a domino effect."

"The butterfly flapping its wings thing?"

"Yes," he said, sweeping her hair from her shoulder to kiss the flesh he revealed. "I make a good choice in one room and the house is secure for everyone."

"You make a bad choice, and it all tumbles down. How do you sleep with the stress?"

"I don't do stress," he said, kissing her neck, her jaw, her ear.

She sank lower to lie down, and his mouth stayed the course, moving with her. "Everyone does stress. It doesn't make you less of a man to feel stress. And suppressing it is not good for your body."

"You think there's something wrong with my body?"

That curled her lips. As he swayed over her, his drowsy eyes drank in the sight.

"Nothing I can see." Her nails met his hips and tickled higher. Somehow, he'd got himself between her thighs again. "Do you think it's possible to know someone you've never met?"

Whatever that meant.

But this didn't feel new.

It did, in all the most sumptuous ways, but the way he slid into her, how his eyes seemed aroused and concerned all at the same time. It was like he cared. But he couldn't. Could he? Did she care about him?

When the sun rose, they'd return to their lives, and this would be a dream, a fantasy, a figment of her imagination. Reliving the memories would never do the night justice. It wasn't over and already it felt unreal.

"I know you," he murmured like he could read her mind. Pushing higher, he drove himself in hard and her mouth opened in a silent gasp. "I know just how to get you off."

And that should be all she wanted from him. Sex. Gratification. Climax. Shit, hormones had a lot to answer for. She wasn't going to be the dumb little coed who fell for the sophisticated man, but he was so different from any guy in her past.

College was college. Work came with its own pitfalls. Usually, business involved much older men making promises they'd never deliver on for a quick fumble. She'd never been that woman. Never fallen for bullshit.

This didn't feel like bullshit. But why? How was this moment any different? Because he didn't want anything from her and hadn't made any promises. It was a night. Like he'd said about life, they were just passing through each other's journeys. After their tryst, they'd never see each other again.

FIVE

"TAKE IT TO SIXTEEN," he said into the phone. Wearing only his shirt, her hair still wet from the shower, she stood picking at what they'd left on the room service cart. "Yes, down…" Nibbling a crouton, she peeked at him. "I know that. I don't give a shit… Just get it done, Greg." He hung up and tossed the phone to the nightstand. "Sorry. Where were we?"

"I don't give a shit, just get it done," she mimicked him and snagged another crouton. "That was hot."

"Yeah, I know, it was my voicemail. I'm showing off for you."

"Funny, 'cause I'm sure I heard it ring," she teased, knowing he was playing with her.

He pushed himself back to sit in the middle of the bed, leaning on the headboard. "You still hungry? We can order whatever you want. Lobster? Caviar?"

While he was ready to move on, she still had questions about the call. "Is it arrogance or puffery?"

"Both," he said.

She picked up the wine and poured what

remained into a glass they'd already used. "That's why I could never be in charge of anything, I don't have the patience for it."

"You don't need patience to be at the top," he said, a smile slowly curving his lips. "You do need patience to stay there."

"I suppose…" Picking up the glass by its rim, she enjoyed the way his gaze flirted with hers while she drank. It kept on going, even as she lowered the glass and sashayed over. "If you're a dick, there would be a coup."

"Having a reputation as a hardass is not a bad thing. Patience doesn't mean pushover. Never be the guy who blinks first."

Kneeling on the bed, she kept going until she straddled his hips again. "You need the goods to back it up." She sipped, then handed him the wineglass. "Do you like being in charge?"

"Yes."

Quick. Clear. No apology.

"There's that arrogance again."

"Honesty, not arrogance. I'm not going to tell you I fell into it by accident. I've been doing this for over a decade. Every day is something else. Every day you have to believe in what you're doing, and that you're capable, or you'll never achieve your goals."

"And your goal is to take over the planet?"

"One business at a time."

He finished the wine and reached over to put it aside. At the same moment, his phone made a sound.

When he turned it over, she read the news app notification on the screen. "Zairn Lomond in sordid sixsome scandal." He laid the device down again. "Sordid, huh? At what point does something become a scandal? At what point does it become an orgy?"

His palms skimmed up and down her arms. "Knowing Zairn, he was the only guy there."

"And that makes a difference?" she asked. "Do you know him?"

"Zairn Lomond? We've crossed paths."

"You want to tell me more about your goals?"

"Goals are important. If you want to get somewhere, you have to know the landmarks on your route."

"So it's one big goal or a lot of little goals?"

"Both. I have an overarching idea of where I want to be. Sometimes I have to think on my feet and pivot here or there, but that's the point of being in charge. Someone has to make decisions fast."

"Be bold," she said, stroking his torso. "Resolute. Unerring."

"Exactly."

"Like inviting strange women to your hotel suite?"

A laugh joined his next smile. "Like I said, this isn't something I do often."

"Does it work though?"

His head tilted as his eyes flicked down. "Uh, yeah, haven't I proved that yet?"

She shoved his shoulder, recognizing his amusement. "I mean does it work in your personal life? The overarching goal thing?"

"That's one riddle I haven't figured out yet."

"Life?"

"Women."

"You do okay," she said, sliding her hands up his body. "We're not that difficult to figure out."

"Every time I think I've got it down, another one of you throws me for a loop."

"Maybe if you prioritized the women in your life, the way you do business, it wouldn't be so hard. Men are the real puzzle."

"Oh, I beg to differ."

"You are! Things can be going great. You're getting closer, having amazing sex, and then suddenly it's over."

"I don't know about that."

"You must have seen it. In life, in your family, do you have siblings?"

"Little sister."

"Men break hearts and don't even blink," she said. "Then they're just onto the next girl like nothing ever happened."

"We're not always unaffected. Usually, we're better at hiding it."

"Not when the guy's the one who ended it. If he wanted a woman that bad, why would he break up with her? Are you really telling me you've never gone brotherly on some guy who broke your sister's heart?"

"No," he said on a snicker. "I haven't. We compete for the same meat." She frowned. "She's gay." Her open mouth rounded in understanding. "Had your heart broken, Siren?"

"I've seen it enough in my friends that I make a point of not getting that close."

"Makes you wonder why we were built so different."

"Men are programmed to spread their seed. Is that your argument?"

"Didn't know I needed an argument."

She landed her hands on his shoulders to push away and lay down next to him. "People need to treat each other as equals. We're all human. There's no excuse for disrespect."

Sliding down onto his side, he supported his head on a fist. "No, there is not. Do you feel disrespected?"

The weighty warmth of his hand on her belly awoke her hormones again.

"At least we know why sex is so fun," she said, tracing her fingertip around each of his fingers as if tattooing them on her skin. "Without it, humanity would be doomed."

"Maybe it is an apology from our higher power."

As he rose on top of her again, she draped her arms around his neck. "Sorry for creating you to drive each other crazy. Here's a reward for putting up with it?"

"Maybe," he said and kissed her.

"Do you believe in a higher power?"

He kissed her again, then met her eye. "No."

"Me either. We're so cynical these days."

He tasted her neck, her jaw, around to her throat. That heat inside her spread until her hips were moving, arching up, looking for something. For him. Inside her.

"Not cynical about this," he said, parting the edges of her shirt to feast on her breasts. "About how fucking bad I need you."

Her legs locked around him, but he kept himself there, too low to join their bodies. "JD," she whimpered when he continued lower.

Where was he going? The question got its answer when he kissed her clit. Damnit, her hips rose and fell, undulating against the motion of his tongue swirling and sucking her clit. How did he do both at the same time like that? How could he—

His tongue plunged into her and she yelped. Fuck, that was deep. It moved in and out of her a few times, then glided back up to her clit. Mm, that tingle, the insistent buzz that built behind it. The pressure cranked up as his speed increased. Shit, then his tongue was inside her again.

Grabbing his head, she tried to force his mouth up, but he resisted and kept on tongue-fucking her with a snicker on his breath. Oh, the asshole meant to drive her crazy. But shit, that was good. Too good.

"JD," she gasped, her fingers still in his hair. "Oh, shit, fuck…" A long, loud yelp leaped from her as orgasm smashed against her. And he kept on going, licking, sucking, pampering her through the first wave and the one that followed. "Ah—" So intense that it was almost pain, she wanted it. Fuck, yes, she wanted it. "JD!"

She huffed through the torment until it gradually subsided. Her chest still rose and fell with the panting of her breath when he kissed her temple.

"How was that for an apology?"

Her lips curled. "For your gender?" she asked, a whisper of a laugh leaving her satisfied lips. "Not too bad."

"We're not all losers who don't know how to satisfy women."

"Is that what it is?" It took actual effort to roll her head on the pillow and look at him through eyes still narrowed in bliss. "Only losers break women's hearts?"

"You intimidate them, Siren. You're beautiful, smart, talented, funny."

"You don't know if I'm talented."

"I can tell by looking at you."

"Are you putting the moves on me?"

"Maybe I am." His hand slid onto her breast, reminding them both it was a little late for the pickup routine. "Real men want their women to excel. They want to build them up, not tear them down. Don't tar us all with the frat boy brush. You're young, there's so much more out there for you to seek, to experience. And it's not all bad."

"Yeah, okay, grandpa," she said, pushing him to his back to climb onto him.

"I'm just saying," he said, laughing as he brushed her hair from her face to hold it at the sides of her head. "You're a beautiful, tenacious woman. The guy who catches you will be lucky to keep up. Don't ever sell yourself short, Siren. Take it from a guy who's been around the world. There are women who can handle it, whatever life throws at them, and they keep on going. Just as there are women who crumble at the first hurdle. On that level, we're the same, men and women."

"The users and the do-ers."

"Something like that."

She licked her lips slow before kissing him. A man who'd been around the world. JD was savvy, and there was a peace to him too. Not just with who he was and what he did, but there was no urgency, no harried desperation that spoke of a man close to the edge.

Yes, there had to be pressure at his level, but no one would know it by looking at him.

She eased back to meet his eye. "JD," she said, catching her breath.

"What is it, baby?" he asked, stroking her hair again.

"Do you think you'll remember this?" Or would she be one in a long line of random one-night stands throughout his life? "Remember me?"

His blink was slow, drowsy, and damnit, she loved the intimacy enveloping them. "No doubt about it. I'll hold every other night against this one. I guarantee none of them will compete. You've broken me, Siren."

Did he want to be broken? Like so many other things he said, she didn't really get it, but it sounded good. And him, he felt good. Giving herself to the pleasure was inevitable. They'd crossed lines with each other, and no one would ever know it. The night was theirs, and theirs alone.

SIX

HER OTHER SHOE. Where was her other shoe? Not under the bed. Not behind the drapes.

"Where are you going?"

Whipping around in response to JD's voice, the sight of him in only a towel, skin glistening, hair damp, she forgot how to breathe for a second.

Swallowing, she pasted on a smile. "You shouldn't be allowed to talk to women when you look like that."

"Get back in bed and I'll let you take advantage."

"The sun has risen, life goes on."

"You going to give me your number?"

Her lips curled into something more genuine until a laugh laced her words. "Come on, JD, you're not going to call."

"I'll call."

"You spend your life on the road."

"I have offices in New York and Boston."

"You're never there." As per their conversations the previous night. "And I live in the Pacific Northwest.

Not exactly a trip down the block."

"I want to visit you."

She sighed. "Why? There's no future here. We both knew that. Do you see me waiting by the phone, desperate for you to call?"

"It wouldn't be like that—"

"And the next time you're in a bar in some hotel somewhere in the world, and a beauty catches your eye?"

"You say that like women are sport. I told you I don't do this. I haven't done this—"

"Because you just got out of a relationship. I'm your rebound," she said, creeping closer. "I'm the woman who gets the last one out of your system so you can move on. It's time to move on, JD."

His brows descended. "And you're not interested in being a part of that future?"

"What do I know about the future or where I want to be? Didn't you say I was a kid? I've never got a relationship to work when I see the guy every day. And the long distance thing? Those girls in college, the ones who'd crow about the boyfriend they had back home, they all ended up with broken hearts. Not one of those relationships made it."

"You think I'm some hick nobody who'll let you down?"

"I think…" she said, going over to lay her hands on his chest, "we had an incredible night. One I won't forget in a hurry. But you're a go-getter and I'm just getting started. Don't you think it's better to have a great memory than to hang on until it falls apart?" He just looked down his nose, considering her. She laughed. "You have no obligation here. Most women probably want promises and roses. I am not one of those women."

"Pragmatic."

"Practical. Yes. I don't create issues for myself. This is not our epic love and we're never going to get married. So what would be the point?"

Holding onto something that didn't exist, or trying to fantasize that it did, would end badly for both of them. The night itself was perfect. One of those memories she'd fall back on after life slowed down later. When she looked back to evaluate her journey, experience would make her whatever she became.

And, in truth, JD knew it. She wasn't giving him new information. A lot of guys, the ones who often thought of themselves as decent, didn't want to use a woman for sex and dump her. In many situations, that would work.

"Don't give up those dreams," he said, maybe appreciating being with a realist over an idealist. "Sometimes life surprises you."

"I hope it does."

Pinching her chin between a curled forefinger and his thumb, he raised her mouth to meet his. His kiss was the perfect period at the end of their encounter. Jamison Dawes was a remarkable man. Being a part of his journey, passing through his life, was an honor. One day, maybe, he'd look back and think the same about her.

PLUS
CONSEQUENCES

FROM: Rylee Hampton
TO: Jamison Dawes
CC:
SUBJECT: Read Me. DO NOT DELETE.

JD,

It's taken me this long to find you, please don't delete this. I couldn't get a phone number for you, and it turns out you're impossible to track down in person. No one would let me just saunter up to a bigshot like you. Anyway, the point, sorry. You remember like six months ago you went to that tech expo in Santa Clara? The hotel. The bar. There was a woman in your seat.

Please tell me you remember. You said that you would.

This isn't the best way to tell you, I know. I don't mean to be landing this on you, but there's no other way to do it. I considered not telling you at all. Finding you was such a struggle, like fate didn't want you to know. I had no idea you were a billionaire overachiever. I didn't know that. That's not why I'm telling you. I'm telling you because it's the right thing to do. Because one day we might need you or you might need us and… I wouldn't want you to find out another way if something happened to me or, you know, anything.

I can't tell you how many times I've talked myself into and out of this. Writing the word is difficult. You must think I'm some kind of nut rambling away. Six months go by without a word. We went our separate ways, and that was supposed to be that.

It was that. Finished. Except it wasn't. That higher power you mentioned has a cruel sense of humor. You said I put myself in your path and I'm about to do it again. Don't take that to mean I want anything from you. I don't. This is merely an exchange of information.

It would be good to know you got this message. So I know you know. Which I guess means I have to say it. Okay. Here goes. I'm pregnant.

Is there a word a guy dreads hearing more? Probably not. I can't say I was over the moon when I found out either. I wasn't sad or angry, just shocked. I think I still am to be honest. As it turns out, it's twins. Congratulations. Shit, I don't mean that to come across wrong. You're entitled to be mad, but you have to know I didn't do this on purpose. There's no way I could've known.

Again, please, be assured, I don't want anything. Not a cent. If you want to be a part of their lives, that's something we can talk about. This is not about money. One day they'll be old enough to ask who their father is. I don't want to lie. I don't want them living in the dark. The whole wide world doesn't need to know. They'll have my last name, and I haven't told anyone, not a soul. No one needs to know. I don't have siblings and my parents are gone. Well, my mom's gone, and I haven't seen my father for years.

That's not important. This is all you have to know: you're going to be a father to twins. A boy and a girl. You hit the jackpot twice in one night.

You probably don't feel very lucky right now and you have the right to discuss this with the people in your life. Equally, if you want to delete this and forget you ever read it, I'll understand. I won't put you on the birth certificate. There won't be child support. I'm capable and happy to raise our children alone. I've been doing it for six months. Already they are my priority. Once you get over the shock, it will be easier to deal with. It's a switch in mindset, but, sorry, you don't have to think about that.

I wanted to tell you and to say thank you. These children are my life. I'll make them my life. It wasn't intentional, but I can't call my babies an accident. For some reason, this happened, and I'll deal with it.

Reply if you want to talk about this. If I never hear from you again, I'll accept that and won't pursue or embarrass you. Thank you for reading this.

—Rylee Hampton

EQUALS

ONE

COFFEE. COOKIES. Damn, she was an idiot.

It was the middle of the afternoon, but who wanted cookies? What was she, like, a ninety-year-old offering the kiddies snacks? This wasn't a cookie meeting. She picked up the plate and scarfed one down on the walk to the kitchen. They wouldn't fit back in the packet, they—

A knock at the door raised her head. Shit. This was it. He was here.

Drawing in a deep breath, she faced the inevitable and opened the front door. "J—" Except it wasn't the man she expected it to be. The two suits on the apartment's threshold were strangers. "Are you lost?"

"Rylee Hampton?"

"Yeah," she said, unsure if that was the right answer.

When the two barreled in, she regretted her agreement. Passing by her kitchen, they planted themselves on her armchair and couch. The latter opened a briefcase on his lap and produced a stack of documents.

If they were so set up, why was she still standing with the door open? Other than just being dumbfounded by their entitlement, one thing was missing.

She glanced out into the hallway. "Where's JD?"

"Mr. Dawes won't be joining us."

Okay, then there was no need for her to be still clutching the door handle. She swung the wood back into the frame and rested a hand on her stomach.

Armchair guy typed into his phone while the paperwork guy noted something in his briefcase and closed it to put it aside.

"I got an email from his account setting this up."

"He's a busy man, Ms. Hampton. This is just a formality."

"A formality?" She drifted toward the couch. Starched, flat affect, but for a glimmer of suspicion, she had this guy pegged. "You're a lawyer."

"Yes, I am."

"And that," she said, nodding at the document in his hand. "Is what?"

"A thorough contract."

"Stating…? That I waive my right to child support?" Sitting down, she smoothed her skirt. Apparently, armchair guy didn't have a purpose other than to just sit there. "I'm not interested in money."

"You will receive child support. Generous. More than generous child support." At least he wasn't going to fight her on— "Pending confirmation of a paternity test."

She smiled. "I figured that one was coming."

Not like she could be offended. They'd met and gone to bed with each other the same night. For all JD and his cronies knew, she did the same thing every day of the week. With him being rich and all, he'd be the best guy to peg parentage on if she was a gold digger.

"It's inescapable and sensible."

"I agree." When her hand stopped on her stomach again, his gaze flicked down and back to the motion. "In my email," which he'd no doubt read, "I said I don't want anything from JD. If he doesn't want to be a part of his children's lives, that's his call."

"Mr. Dawes believes in family. He's a man of integrity."

"His children shouldn't be an obligation. We had one night, it was fun. I didn't expect this either. Following through with this pregnancy is my choice. I have no problem doing this myself and leaving him off the birth certificate."

"Good, then there won't be any reason not to sign this."

He slid up the couch to hand her the outstretched document.

"Wow, weighty."

It was maybe only ten pages, but when it came to her kids' lives, even without meeting them in the flesh, their well-being was all that mattered.

"There's nothing in there meant to trick you. No clause that says you have to repay child support in the event of… It's a simple transaction. Mr. Dawes will pay monthly support toward the upbringing of these children. In exchange, he's entitled to one weekend a month visitation."

"And where will that visitation take place?" she asked, flicking through the papers. "I don't want them bundled on a jet to God knows where without knowing he'll bring them back."

"Again, that's written into the contract. All duties are covered. He will not take them out of the lower forty-eight without written permission from you." Wow, really? The guy she'd met in that bar was not a reasonable "*written permission*" kind of person. "Likewise, you cannot take them from the lower forty-eight without Mr. Dawes' explicit written permission."

Ah, gotcha. Yeah. That made more sense. So it was erasing any hint of a double standard, she could appreciate that. Obviously, Mr. Dawes didn't want her disappearing with the twins and probably had no intention of taking them anywhere himself. Why vacation with two hungry, demanding children when the alternative was loading up a yacht with supermodels and disappearing for a month? What a way to unwind.

"If he can't show up for this meeting, how do I know he'll show up for the kids? Does he have experience caring for children?"

She didn't exactly have bags of it herself, but she'd be Mom from the minute they were born. Not only would she have on-the-job training, she'd also gone to classes and read every book and scoured websites touting tips and tricks. If JD couldn't show up to discuss visitation, it wasn't likely he'd be pulling all-nighters to bone up on how to change a diaper.

"Mr. Dawes' mother will take responsibility for the children when he is unable to fulfill the commitment."

Polite as this lawyer was trying to be, did he know that using words like "commitment" and "duties" in relation to her children pissed her off?

"So he wants visitation he doesn't plan to show up for? Our children are…"

With that, she inhaled and closed her mouth. Whatever kind of mother she hoped to be, it wasn't her place to tell JD what kind of father he should be. That was up to him. All she could do was her best and focus on her own relationship with the twins. The one thing she wouldn't do was let JD's picture of parenting influence hers, or her bond with the babies.

"Ms. Hampton?"

"Child support," she said, turning to the appropriate page. "That's too much. Two children, yes, defray costs, yes. They do not need sports cars and prize ponies from the minute they're born. Half it, at least."

"Okay," the lawyer said, producing a pen from an inside pocket. "I'll take that to him. Anything else?"

"I haven't read the whole thing. It would be smart to have my lawyer look over it."

"You have a lawyer?"

No. Not yet. But she'd figure it out. "I can get a lawyer."

"Okay. Do you believe Mr. Dawes is trying to trick you?"

"No," she said. "But this is a big deal, it's my children's lives. I don't know what I'm looking for in a contract like this."

"Pick one."

"Pick—what?"

"Go online, find a lawyer, pick whoever you want."

"I don't understand what—"

"This has to be done today. Pick someone you feel comfortable with and Mr. Dawes will cover all costs. Do you have a computer?"

Yes, she had a computer. "What's the rush?"

"We're only in town today."

Okay, yeah, they wouldn't want to hang around indefinitely waiting for this to be done. Some might say there was no hurry, but, at seven months, these babies could come any time. Wasn't her fault it took six months to track down a way to get hold of the guy. Men like Dawes got things done. His lawyer would need the same mentality.

She went to the bedroom to retrieve her laptop and put it on the kitchen counter to boot it up. Her feet hurt. Damn, but there was no way she could sit with it on her lap, the kids would get in the way.

"I don't think that just anyone will be available at a moment's notice. Are we going to their office? They'll need time to review—"

"Whoever you want will come immediately," the lawyer said, leaving the couch to come join her.

"Because you say so?"

"Because money talks," he said. "I can negotiate on your behalf, if you would like. But I'd imagine offering a fifty K retainer would get even the laziest lawyer off his or her ass."

For that amount of money, most anyone would jump to action. "Fifty K?"

"Like I said, we have to get this done."

Just like that. He tossed cash around like it was water. "This is JD's money?"

"We have a fund specifically for this kind of thing."

How many secret kids did he have dotted around the country, the world?

"Does he think money fixes everything?"

"He pays me to do the thinking." Producing a card from his inside pocket, he slid it across the counter. "Write your bank details down. I'll transfer the money immediately."

"You'll transfer it to me?"

"Yes. There's no reason your lawyer should know where the funds are coming from. We want impartiality. Prevents you suggesting impropriety down the line."

What did this guy think of her? What had JD told his lawyer about her? She drew the card across the counter to read his name. "Mr. Andrews, don't forget you came to me. I told JD that he could ignore the email and I wouldn't create trouble. Why would that be different now?"

"Now isn't the concern," he said. "This contract protects all of us in perpetuity."

Who knows what the future might bring? If they were covering their bases, she needed to do the same.

TWO

"IT IS VERY CLEAR," Mr. Faulds said. "The restrictions are tight."

"Why does that matter?" she asked.

For an hour, she and her new lawyer had sat in her bedroom trying to figure things out. With him perched on one of her kitchen stools and her on the edge of the bed, this was no cookie meeting either.

JD's people still loitered in her living room. This impromptu consultation couldn't be more bizarre. Mr. Faulds seemed like a decent person. What did she know about lawyers? At least she'd picked him herself.

Damn, her back was aching. If she didn't move soon, she'd be immobile for the rest of the day. Propping her hands on the mattress behind her, she tried to lever the pressure from her spine.

"It matters a great deal because there are penalties if you reveal the identity of your child's father."

"They can sue me for whatever they want. I don't have anything to give." Billionaire moguls sure didn't need her measly savings. "And I have no intention of telling anyone who the father is."

"You don't have family?" They'd already discussed that. Apparently, this guy was thorough to the point of driving her crazy. "Friends? A boyfriend?"

"No one knows, not even my OB."

His attention returned to the document in his lap. "Child support is generous."

"I've told them we don't need that much. I'm not looking to score here. JD and I were a one-night deal. This is not about money."

"That may be the case, but have you read the visitation clauses?"

Had she read them? Maybe. Did that mean she got all the legalese? No.

"What about visitation?"

"Marjorie Dawes, Jamison's mother, lives in Boston. Did you think about that?"

"Did I think about it? Please just tell me what—"

"If you have to send the children across the country once a month, who will cover the cost? An adult will have to travel with them when they're young. If Jamison is unavailable, do you propose his mother, a woman in her fifties, should make the trip every month for the next twenty years?"

Was that her problem? "What do you suggest?"

"That visitation be based here in Seattle."

"I don't understand. Wouldn't she still have to make the trip back and forth?"

"That's up to them," he said. "Either way, the children should remain in this state for regular weekend visitation. How would you feel if Dawes hired a chaperone? A third, unrelated party? Someone you've never met? Perhaps someone he's never met."

Concern moved her head in a shake. "I don't want them with a stranger."

"He'd have to put that guardian under a gag order too. While he's limiting information and exercising control, you are just another of his employees. His children have no choice, and you are not asserting yourself for their benefit. Someone has to focus on their welfare."

Interesting point. "And if I'm not allowed to tell anyone who their father is, how do I explain third-party chaperones and cross-country flights?"

"Perhaps in private jets with unchecked pilots?"

Okay, now the guy was freaking her out. Could be that he'd seen the zeros on his retainer check and wanted more, but she couldn't deny his points were valid.

"We need more certainty."

"Exactly. Let's get rid of those unknown values by being specific."

"It's still a lot to ask of his mother, every month until the kids are…"

By the time they were in their teens, they'd be able to fly themselves. Though she didn't have a lot of faith in the safety of that.

"Dawes has no permanent base. You aren't making this demand of his mother, he is. If he values his time with his children, there's no reason he should miss regular visitation. If he fails to appear, it's him who is putting the pressure on his mother to be here. And you should meet her."

Shock widened her eyes. "His mother?"

"It's inevitable."

"Meeting my one-night stand's mother?"

"If she has an active role in your children's lives, your paths will cross. You will have to hand the children off to her. Meeting now allows us to add any stipulations before the contracts are signed."

"Andrews wants it done today."

Mr. Faulds smiled. "No, Ms. Hampton. No ink

will touch paper today. Their urgency alone should be enough of a concern for us to slow this down. Your children aren't going anywhere."

Andrews would regret the decision to provide her with counsel. Maybe Faulds planned to gouge her for whatever he could get, but she wouldn't object to being thorough.

"No." Her hand moved to her bump. "But there is a deadline."

"Not exactly. You said in your email to Mr. Dawes that you were happy to raise the children without his input."

"Yes."

"And that you plan to omit him from the birth certificate."

"Yes. I don't want my children at risk and it's my choice to have them. No one else's."

"So technically…" he said, his eyes meeting hers with a kind of knowing, "whatever we give them by way of visitation is a gift. You are not obliged to give Mr. Dawes any kind of access."

"I don't want this to get dirty. At the end of the day, he is their father, and it's not my place to damage or deny that relationship."

"That's exactly what he's asking you to do. He wants this to remain a secret and you are giving him the means to do that. You are yielding to him when you hold all the cards. Why?"

"If this gets to court, it will get messy."

Not that it wasn't already chaos. Chaos… it's just mathematics.

"Ideally, we don't want to end up in front of a judge."

She clicked back to the moment. "Hmm?"

"I was saying we don't want to end up in front of a judge."

"No, we don't. Because, no offense to you, but JD would throw a helluva lot more money at this than I can." And maybe he'd find a way to take the twins from her completely. "You're right. We don't want to rush this."

"At this stage, we need time to ruminate. To redline this draft and counter their proposal. This is the first inning, Ms. Hampton. It's not unusual for these things to go back and forth for a while, sometimes years."

"We don't have years. And Andrews says he's only in town today."

"Did you know the man he brought with him is a notary?"

"No, we weren't introduced."

"Don't allow yourself to be dismissed or intimidated. We'll get this right, Ms. Hampton. Find a way to make everyone happy."

"Andrews won't like delays."

"Their terms are specific. That puts us in a strong position."

"How so?"

"This contract lays out everything they want. What's the harm in ensuring you get what's best for your children?"

Nothing. This guy was good.

"Okay," she said, groaning as she boosted herself up. Mr. Faulds was gentleman enough to take her arms to help put her on her feet. "Let's go tell them the good news."

THREE

AS MUCH SENSE as her lawyer, Faulds, made, she couldn't say the meetings and hour-long calls were a highlight of her week. Since Andrews left her apartment in a snit with his notary, there had been a dozen video conferences. New faces. New lawyers appeared in every one. On the other side, of course. Faulds was sticking with her. Fifty grand bought loyalty, apparently.

Intimidation tactics, that's how Faulds explained the beefed-up opposition. Good for them. She'd never pegged JD as the type to hide behind others. So she was wrong. Wouldn't be the first time. Imagine, it could be that the morning she left his suite might be the last time she ever laid eyes on the guy. No phone call. No email. He was never in the meetings. His kids were low on his agenda. That was a message delivered loud and clear, and she couldn't care less. It was his loss and there were more important considerations in her life.

Her OB had told her to take it easy. Bedrest was the recommendation. The kids got bigger every day, sometimes every damn minute. Each morning, it got just a little harder to get out of bed. An expert at bounce and swing, she dreaded to think what would happen on the day she eventually failed to swoop herself onto her feet.

Dreaded thoughts of labor often eclipsed her excitement about meeting her children. Trepidation grew. Just how was she supposed to do it? As an abstract thought, it was fine, but they were creeping closer to inevitable parenthood. Two children. She had to push two children out of her body and then take complete responsibility for their safety.

Which was worse?

That answer swung back and forth too.

At the end of the workday, all she wanted to do was get home, soak her feet, and eat. Didn't matter what. Just eat. And pee. She had to pee. Damn kids had her running back and forth to the restroom all day. Already they liked to bicker and push each other around. She'd get on that, you know, get them in line. After their birth. Punishing them before might lead to a little payback in the labor suite. And just how did someone discipline children in utero?

Ah, the lights of her life.

"Excuse me."

In the Spotlight Solutions lobby, her path intersected another woman's. Maybe about her age, the redhead carried confidence like she'd never seen.

"Uh, is something wrong?"

"I…"

The woman glanced over her shoulder at a woman at the edge of the space. With everyone else moving, on their way to somewhere, the woman's stillness was stark.

There was that trepidation again. When the redhead's gaze met hers, she exhaled.

"You have the same eyes."

"Good," the woman said, beaming. "His

obviously worked to get you into bed. Great odds on my chance for a Dawes follow-up."

Her shoulders dropped. All the tension became something like relief, and she laughed.

Oh, the inevitable came in many forms. "What do you know about chaos theory?"

That creased the woman's brow. "Chaos theory? Like science?"

"Mathematics," she said.

"Nothing. I know exactly nothing about it."

"Good. You're already miles ahead," she said and cradled her belly. "There's just one little thing in the way."

"Two, I hear."

"True. And they're not so little."

The woman shrugged. "I'll work around 'em." She extended a hand. "Brenna."

"Rylee," she said and they shook.

Rather than let go, Brenna eased her hand closer. "We're family. We just want to be your family, Rylee. These babies mean so much to her." Her? Marjorie Dawes. "Please don't break her heart."

"I don't want to hurt anyone. The more love these kids can have in their lives, the better."

Brenna's smile grew again. "We're going to get along. I can tell already." She put an arm around her. "Come meet our mom."

She resisted. "It's late."

"It's five o'clock… ish."

Fair. Yeah, why else would she be leaving the office? "I have a dinner reservation for three."

"There are three of us."

"No," she said, stroking her stomach. "I'm three."

Brenna peered closer. "Is this you telling me to get lost? Should I get defensive and shouty?"

"No," she said, almost laughing again. Was JD this funny? "This is me saying at thirty-two weeks, if these children don't get fed on time, they get cranky."

The woman's head bobbed in understanding. "They get that from Jamie. Well… less maybe of the fed thing, he just gets cranky."

"You call him Jamie?"

Brenna nodded. "What do you call him?"

Her lips twisted in a badly subdued smile, and she leaned in, still holding her belly. "Nothing that should be repeated around little ears."

"I'll bet." Brenna snickered. "We're not all shoot and run. If I take you to dinner, will you give us a chance?"

"Throw in a restroom stop and I might even listen to what you have to say."

Brenna's attention returned to the twins. "It's really… real."

"Yes, they are." Taking the woman's hand, she held it on her stomach. "They're in there ramping up to a squabble. How do you feel about pizza?"

"Mom has Jamie's credit card. You can have whatever you want."

"Champagne and caviar all round."

"Are you allowed to drink champagne?"

"I didn't say I would drink it, but I have no problem charging him for it."

"Isn't him liquoring you up how you got into this in the first place?"

"Champagne? No." This time she didn't resist when Brenna put an arm around her to guide them across the foyer. "Tequila's responsible for this."

Brenna laughed. "Could be a good name for one of them."

"Yeah, and then we'd never forget."

"How drunk were you?"

"Not drunk enough that I couldn't have walked away." Her lips parted for a breath. "I could've walked away any minute… Until he kissed me anyway. After that, I was all in."

"All in is Jamie's style."

Not with his kids, but that would wait for another time. "That's the past. No more talk of that." She patted her belly. "Let's stick to the future."

RESULT

ONE

LABOR.

She'd be pissed no one prepared her, except she wasn't sure preparation was possible for such a tremendous and traumatic event.

Her children were in the world. Her babies. Her purpose. Her reason for being. Funny how priorities shifted in that first moment of holding them. They'd grown in her body, she knew them, they knew her. It wasn't an introduction or a meeting, it was an acknowledgement that they were in it for the long haul and trusted each other implicitly.

What was her life about? Her reason for being on the earth? These children.

Children she better get back to.

Yeah, okay, so she wasn't supposed to go to the restroom alone, something she'd been doing for most of her life, but the staff would never know.

Or would they?

Someone was sitting on her bed. A guy. With his back to her, peering into the cribs.

Not just any guy.

She wet her lips. "You're in my seat."

He leaped up to turn. "Rylee."

"You expecting someone else, JD?"

"They're—we're—"

"I wasn't sure I'd ever see you again." That particular moment probably wasn't the ideal one to bring it up. Smoothing her nightgown, she rounded the end of the bed. "Have you held them?"

His eyes wide, he recoiled a few inches. "God, no."

"You'll have to do it sometime."

"I wouldn't even know where to…"

Scooping up baby one, she didn't give him a choice. "Put her head in…" The little one whimpered, but her heavy eyes barely moved. "That, Mr. Big Flashy Jamison Dawes, is your daughter." He just stared at her. Frozen. "Sky. Her name's Sky."

"She's… incredible."

"Yes, she is and came in almost two pounds heavier than her brother." Picking up baby two, she kissed his head, holding her lips there for a second before using her hip to roll aside the crib. "Kye."

"Kye?" he asked, stiffening when the little guy was eased into his father's other arm.

"Yes, but we're spelling it K-Y-E, rather than K-A-I."

"Why?"

She plopped herself onto the edge of the bed. "Because I want to."

"Rylee, I—"

"I got you decaf because…" Brenna glided into the room, then stopped dead. "Oh, look who showed up. So you did get mom's message?"

"Don't start with me…" JD began but faltered when Sky grumbled.

"I should take a picture," Brenna said, putting down the coffees and slipping her phone out of her pocket to hold it up. "This might be the only chance I get to prove he was once in the same room as his children."

"Glad your input's so constructive, Nana," JD said, though his frown was probably more to do with the wriggling babies.

His sister wasn't dissuaded and came over to help him out by stealing Kye. "He has your ears. Poor little guy."

He scowled. "My ears? What does that even mean?"

"I don't know, Jamie. It's something people say, I'm saying it." Fussing over the baby, Brenna's kissy faces were just too cute. "We're keeping him away from you. We don't want him imprinting on a guy who's never around."

"I'm here."

"Because mom called you."

"How else would I have known?"

"You're a deadbeat dad," Brenna said without hesitation.

"I'm earning money to support them."

"Okay, go do that then, and we'll support them with love." Kye's aunt kissed the end of his nose. "Won't we, little guy? Yes, we will."

"You want to give us a minute, Brenna," JD said, putting Sky back in her crib.

"Put her feet at the bottom," she said, pouncing off the bed to check her daughter's position.

"Why do you need a minute?"

"Bren."

The siblings made eye contact before Brenna sought the nod from her. She could handle JD.

"Can I take the babies with me?"

"No," JD said, stepping in to relieve his sister of Kye. The guy was a quick study. "Give the woman back her child."

"Her child?" Brenna asked, sauntering toward the door. "Mom thinks you should get married, by the way."

"Yes, thank you." JD went over to open the door and push his sister out before closing it again. "I'm sorry about her."

"I like your sister," she said, tucking her boy back in. "She doesn't take herself too seriously."

"She doesn't take anything seriously."

"I don't think that's fair," she said. "In a fair fight for meat, I'm surprised you ever won."

"Something to do with the penis."

She turned. "Your one redeeming quality."

Their eyes met. "Apparently so." He took a breath. "You want to get married?"

Wouldn't that be hilarious?

Her smile flared. "No."

"Didn't think you would."

"You did nothing wrong," she said, stepping closer to take his hand at his side. "Neither of us intended for this to happen and it doesn't change anything." He frowned. "Okay, so it changes things, but nothing between us. My relationship with my children is separate from your relationship with them. Providing we both agree not to put them in the middle or bitch about each other in front of them, we won't compel each other to do anything."

"You think it's that simple?"

"Do you want me calling you every time I run out of diapers? Every time one of them sneezes? Every time—"

"I get it."

"Your mom is great."

"She's moving to Seattle."

"Yes," she said. "I can't argue with her priorities."

"I'd appreciate it if you'd…" He cleared his throat. "Let her be their grandmother."

She smiled again. "She is their grandmother, JD. I won't get in the way of any family relationships with the twins, so long as they're not damaging. And she's been there for them, caring for them, for a month."

While they were in her belly but it still counted.

"Unlike me."

She held up both hands in surrender. "Nothing to do with me. You do you, JD. The rest of us will be just fine. If you choose to be an absent father—"

"I'm not absent."

"A part-time, wham-bam parent, whatever. You're a busy man."

"I didn't factor this into…"

Frustrated though he looked, it was kind of amusing. "Think any of us did? Like I said, your relationship with them is your business." Still, the weight of the world was on him. That grumpy, perplexed look on his face sort of reminded her of Kye. "Your children will be looked after. They will be loved."

"They need their father."

"So be there for them. Whenever you can, however you can. That doesn't have to mean sitting by them every minute. You're building their legacy, right?"

That switched on a light behind his eyes. "Their legacy."

The kids would decide in time if they wanted to be a part of their father's ever-expanding empire. If they stole him away from what he loved, he'd only grow to resent them. Who knew how any of their relationships would turn out? The kids might resent him for any absence, or they could despise her for making the rules.

Nothing was certain.

A single knock on the door came before it opened, and a young guy came in. "Hello, I'm from…"

He touched the ID card clipped to his belt.

"The lab," she said, figuring it out. Best to get it over and done with. "Okay, do what you have to do. Works out everyone's here. Do you need their blood?"

She didn't want her babies to be hurt but wasn't wild about anyone sticking things in their sensitive mouths either.

"Who is this guy?" JD asked, back to that affront. "Is there something wrong?"

"Paternity," she said, sitting on the bed again. "Open wide, Daddio."

ONE

PRESENT DAY

SEVEN YEARS Rylee Hampton had worked for Spotlight Solutions. Seven years. Damn, that sounded like a lot. More than a lifetime for some people. A creative consultant in the marketing department, part of a large team, she spent most of her time sketching other people's ideas.

At the end of the day, everyone was ready to go home, her included. They'd been ready until, less than an hour ago, an unexpected email hit her department's inbox, scuppering any chance of getting out on time. The message summoned an array of employees to the biggest conference space on the first floor. Usually reserved for product launches, corporate events, or visiting speakers, it rarely got aired out. If the three hundred or so other people in the room were an accurate indication, other departments had got the same message at the last minute as well.

What was the impromptu meeting about? God

knew. But she wasn't worried. The corporation's competent infrastructure had undergone a couple of facelifts through the years. So far, she'd survived the layoffs. Loyalty bought her consideration, or so she liked to think. Rumors persisted about the direction of the company, more so recently, but she'd switched off to them a long time ago. Without a reliable link to anyone close to the top, it was impossible to figure out what was truth and what was fiction. Theories changed and became more embellished every week. The tide always rose. In time, it would fall again. Riding the Spotlight rapids was part of everyday life.

Others weren't so apathetic. Her marketing colleagues' mumbles and the rumble of surrounding conversation conveyed confusion and intrigue. The room was alive with questions and speculation. When was the last time she'd been in that room? The Christmas party? Maybe the mock expo. Damn, she wanted to go home, but there they were, waiting for the CEO to show up for some unknown reason.

There had to be some big announcement. Had to be. That could be the only explanation for bringing so many people together and keeping it hush-hush until the eleventh hour. Couldn't be that important if they were leaving everyone swinging in the wind. The raucous conversation continued as people waited for something to happen on the dais at the head of the room.

People loved to gossip, but there was a thread of fear in the excited tone swirling around her. In the current economic climate, everyone wanted to hold on to their jobs. Big changes could mean big cuts. Redundancies, budgets, departments were already stretched thin.

Nichelle leaned in at her side to whisper, "Here comes Ted."

Their CEO. The sooner he got started, the closer

she'd be to home.

Of her marketing colleagues, Nichelle was the closest thing she had to a friend in the department. Though, in truth, her life outside of work was more important than her job. A social life, being "in" with her colleagues, was unimportant, so she wasn't particularly close to any of them.

Polite and civil, she didn't have deep relationships at Spotlight. She kept her head down, did her job, and went home to the life that she loved.

From behind the dais, Ted ascended the stairs to the prominent spot at the central podium. Other members of the board shuffled onto the stage behind him.

"Everyone!" Ted called. "Everyone settle down!"

Always jovial with a smile on his face, Ted was a good boss, though not the smartest of businessmen. Word among employees implied he was understanding and generous. He didn't have the cutthroat spirit needed to close the deals that would ensure the corporation's, thus the employees', futures. Which was better? A superior who listened in the short term or one focused on the bigger picture?

She'd only met the man once, at a function in that very room. They'd spoken for a second. He wouldn't remember her, but she'd got a good sense from him, a good energy.

Ted tapped the microphone as the room settled down and the board seated themselves.

"Thank you, everyone, for coming today," Ted said, setting his hands on the podium. "I know this is spur-of-the-moment; you have jobs you want to get back to or homes to get to. It's been a long day, so I'll make this brief. I'm sure many of you have heard the rumors about Spotlight Solutions and our financial troubles."

Redundancies.

Budget cuts.

The words rattled in her head.

So much for not being worried.

Tension gripped the room. It clenched her guts too. If this news related to downsizing, she could be in big trouble. Her four-bedroom apartment was already more than she should be able to afford.

"Oh God," Nichelle said and took her hand, eyes locked on the stage.

"Please nobody panic," Ted said and widened his grin. "We've been in secret negotiations for some time now and finally the day has come to say we have been rescued." The room relaxed somewhat, but still held its breath. "Spotlight Solutions has been purchased. I know it's unexpected, but the buyout secures everyone's jobs and our future projects." The room applauded. Ted held up his hands. "Please, everyone, save your applause for our savior, Mr. Jamison Dawes!"

Uh, what did he just say?

People kept applauding when a new person jogged up the stairs at the back of the stage. The man unknown to the room held up his hands to silence the crowd, presumably to introduce himself.

Oh, fuck. Jamison Dawes wasn't unknown to her. They needed no introduction. Her mouth dried as it fell open. What the hell was he doing there? What did he think he was doing?

The applause died down.

JD went to the podium to shake Ted's hand. All very posed and perfect, like politicians accepting the nomination for something. Oh, steam should be coming out of her ears. Despite being such a prominent feature of her life, it had been a while since they'd laid eyes on each other. The last place she'd expected to see him was at her workplace.

Ted backed away to take a seat with the other board members. And she couldn't snap out of it.

Wearing that dashing smile, JD settled the room. Been a long time since she'd seen that smile too. That damn smile that tipped the first domino; they'd been falling ever since. Crashing into each other, one after another, with an inevitability she'd almost come to rely on.

He charmed every person in the place. "Thank you. Thank you, everyone."

Known as a shrewd businessman, personable and generous, JD was a good man, and extremely successful in his field. Good at lots of things, he was a philanthropist, a mentor, and made headlines gobbling up corporations around not only the country but the world.

Whatever he was saying, she heard none of it over the ringing in her ears. He could've recited *War and Peace* and she still wouldn't have had time to snap out of her daze.

A rushing of air overtook the ringing. Oh, a storm was coming. Seeing him up there, in front of her colleagues, *her* colleagues, talking, commanding attention, it was too much to take in.

Surreal was a better word. Too surreal for her to absorb.

The father of her children, that was his category in her life. A category that had nothing to do with her career. Their sparse direct contact happened through phone conversations and emails. Most communication was done by way of his mother, the conduit for his relationship with their twins. Formal visitation was satisfied by Marjorie Dawes and JD just showed up at his mom's to see the kids when he could.

Dumbfounded, she couldn't place him there, in her life, in her workplace. Spotlight had been hers, and only hers, and now he was there.

Why?

Shit, sitting only half a dozen rows from the front of the room had been a mistake, though not one she could've planned for. JD finished his speech and stepped back to accept the adoring applause. Waving, he scanned the space. Damnit. Damnit. His gaze went right past her. Thank God. Relief. A reprieve. He'd missed her.

But she'd breathed out too soon.

His attention stopped and returned to seek out… In a sea of faces, shouldn't she be invisible? What was she worrying about? He wouldn't—

Nope, he fixated right on her. Embarrassing that he seemed to be trying to place her, like he couldn't quite figure out her identity. The longer it took, the smaller she felt.

It probably only took a few seconds and she shouldn't be offended. Given it wasn't a familiar environment, and they hadn't seen each other for so long, it was no big deal. Right? Shouldn't she forgive him for his second of hesitation? Definitely not her finest moment.

Eventually, he caught on and tilted his head like he was asking why she was there. So sorry for existing. Owner of the damn world, he didn't have to be so cocky. She was where she was supposed to be; he was the one encroaching on her turf. And what the hell could she do about it? Bupkis.

The father of her children had bought the company she worked for and she'd been oblivious to the fact that it was happening. This was going to take some adjustment… and she'd have to call her lawyer before she spoke to anyone about it. Her lips were sealed. Officially.

Ted approached JD's other side and put an arm around him. The men shook hands again. Their current

CEO said another few words. Ted thanked the room for their time and promised further information in due course, whatever that meant. Everyone was dismissed like her world hadn't just rocked on its axis.

Time to skate. When the first people stood, and the conversation level rose again, she leaped to her feet. No hanging around for her.

"I have to go," she said, shuffling past Nichelle.

The other marketing employees happily gossiped, speculating on the direction of the company now that they'd been bought by this savvy hotshot.

Nichelle bent down to grab her own purse. "Wait, Rylee, I'll walk out with you. Wait for me."

At the end of the row, she didn't even care that her hasty pushing pissed others off. Nichelle tried to follow, further irritating their loitering colleagues. Winning friends wasn't on her priority list. If they wanted to be pissed off, they could be pissed off, let them crank up their blood pressures.

"It's okay, Nichelle. I really have to go. I'm already late," she said. "See you tomorrow."

Hurrying out before the masses corked the bottleneck at the doors, she needed out of there in case JD thought to corner her. As far as she was concerned, he could keep his distance forever.

Their rhythm worked for everyone, except him, apparently. Why did he screw with the status quo? The years hadn't dampened his arrogance that was for sure. It might have been attractive when they met, now it was just annoying.

Damnit, she didn't like surprises.

TWO

DREAD OVER THE UNWELCOME surprise chased her home and through dinner. At her kitchen island, chopping carrots into sticks, her mind kept working. What would JD's next move be? Was this a game? What did he want?

The twins would like it if daddy started working in town. How long would it last? His corporate MO: buy a company, spend some time shaping it, then move onto the next one, put an expiration date on her children's happiness. Always expanding his portfolio, JD often spliced companies into parts, keeping some and selling others. For him, it was all about growth… at least that's what his mother told her.

At some point, she'd have to talk to him. Damn. What would she say? Close though she was to Marjorie Dawes, his mother, she didn't want to put the woman in the middle. His sister, Brenna, on the other hand… she'd put herself right smack in the middle and would dare anyone to try moving her. After the kids, her friendship with Brenna was the most important in her life.

It had been anyway. How would that change with him in town?

He'd come in, mix things up, and then ride off into the sunset.

A storm front leaving carnage in its wake. And just like a storm, JD wouldn't notice or care about collateral damage.

Going through the motions, preparing for the following day, her other eye was on her twins seated at the long dinner table to the left of the kitchen island.

"But, Mommy, I eated lots of it," Kye complained.

"You eated less than me," Sky said.

Her four-year-old twins poked at each other's plates, comparing what remained of their dinner portions. Typical siblings, they each had a lot of love for the other and liked to show that by riling each other at every opportunity.

Switching to mommy mode, she cleared her mind. "Ate," she said. "The word you're both looking for is 'ate.' You'll keep on eating until you can both say you *ate* it all."

There was a knock at the front door.

"Is that Grama?" Sky asked, bouncing up high on her knees, desperate to bolt from her chair.

She raised a hand to stall her children, signaling they shouldn't scurry to the door.

"No," she said, rinsing her hands and grabbing a towel. "You'll see Grama tomorrow. It's probably Auntie Brenna."

Both kids deflated with disappointment. Hilarious. Grama would take their side on the finishing their dinner debate, Brenna wouldn't. Their grandmother doted on her grandchildren. Their aunt enjoyed playing with people too much to give anyone an easy out.

Still smiling, she tossed the towel over her

shoulder and went across the apartment to open the front door, expecting to see Brenna.

Instead, JD stood on her threshold. "You have an employee file," he said, which she guessed cleared up the question of how he'd got her address.

Astute, or arrogant, he answered the question before she'd asked it. Brenna and Marjorie had her address. If he'd gone through the employee files rather than asking his relatives, she'd bet that meant his family didn't know he was in town. At least she wasn't the only one blindsided.

Catching her breath, there wasn't much time to gather her wits. "At Spotlight Solutions? Yes, I have an employee file. Know why? Because I work there. And this is not there. This is home, not work. What are you doing here?"

He skipped over the last question. "You work there," he said, but it wasn't really a question. Good, he was supposed to be smart, and they'd clarified her position of employment already. "I had no idea."

Really? The sarcasm drawled through her brain. Spotlight Solutions was a prominent software firm. If he'd wanted something local, it would be the most likely one he'd buy. Not that she'd known it was for sale exactly. Given the company struggles, bet he got it at a good price.

He couldn't have expected to buy Spotlight and keep it secret forever. It wasn't like he'd taken an anonymous position in the mailroom; he would take over as CEO. The person at the top of the pyramid was usually the most recognizable. Had she thought of him as smart?

Somehow, it fell to her to point out the obvious. "We met at a software expo," she said. "It never occurred to you that maybe I worked for a software company?"

JD looked almost baffled. "It never occurred to me to look."

"Of course not."

Speaking fast and matching his pace was a necessity. Talking before thinking things through was typical of them. Stubbornness, and their back-and-forth banter, had drawn them to each other in the first place. Old habits and all that.

They brought out a need in each other to get in the last word, to match each other quip for quip. Mature? No. It was what it was. Honestly, she hated how exciting baiting him could be and how easily she confused their repartee for having fun.

She was supposed to be mad at him, or at least demanding answers. Her heart rate kicking up was nothing more than an increase in adrenaline caused by him aggravating her. That was the reason. The only reason.

A little hand grabbed her knee and pulled at her until a tiny body squeezed around her leg.

"Mommy, I want to see," Sky said, blinking upward.

"You're not supposed to—"

Sky squealed. "Daddy!"

JD bent to scoop her up. "Hello, Sproutette."

Putting her arms around him, Sky glowed, then grabbed his face in both hands. "Did you be missing me?"

"Of course I missed you, sweetheart. You're my angel."

JD kissed the end of their daughter's nose. Though she rolled her eyes and folded her arms, it was kind of cute to see them together. These interactions weren't something she usually got to witness.

"Did you come to see my bedroom?" Sky asked but didn't wait for the inconvenience of an answer.

"Mommy, Daddy wants to see my bedroom."

The kids were his ticket to getting inside the apartment. Not that she was keeping him outside exactly, but he'd tickled her suspicion by avoiding the question of why he'd shown up.

"No, he doesn't," she said and kept going before JD could correct her. "Daddy wants you to sit at the table with Kye to finish your dinner." Sky blinked at her father, giving her mother the chance to glare at him. "Because Daddy would never dare undermine Mommy's authority on something as important as feeding you."

His smirk stayed on their daughter, though it was for her, not the little one. "What are you having for dinner, Sproutette?"

"Pasta," Sky said, screwing up her face.

He gasped. "Oh, wow! Pasta? I love pasta!" he said with more enthusiasm than he would if talking to an adult, but it worked like a dream with Sky.

The grumpy little one quickly reverted to her bubbling joy. "You want some of mines?"

Her kids might think that they were smart, but watching out for their tricks was her full-time job. Sky had seen her father; it would be unfair to keep him from Kye. Sky also wouldn't give her parents peace, meaning she wouldn't get to the bottom of why JD was there, until their daughter was appeased.

She gave in to the inevitable. "Uh, no," she said, entering the apartment, leaving the door open for JD to bring Sky inside. "If Daddy wants to eat with you, Mommy will fix him his own plate. You have to clear yours."

The scrape of her son's chair legs on the slate floor came before the front door even had a chance to close.

"Daddy!" Kye called out.

In a few weeks, their babies would turn five.

Their little bodies needed the help of booster seats to reach the table, but both were professionals at climbing up and down either to get up or to get away.

Returning to her place on the other side of the kitchen island, she hung up the towel but faltered. The vision of JD standing at the foot of the dining table, holding both children, sent her mind back to the hospital on the day the kids were born. That was probably the last time she'd seen him holding them both together. Babies then, both considerably smaller, JD didn't make it look any more difficult now than it had been all those years ago.

Shaking off the moment of sentiment, she cleared her throat. What had she been doing before he showed up to disrupt their lives?

"You had to come at dinnertime when I'm trying to get them both to eat, didn't you?"

Their inability to give each other a break was mutual. She didn't expect him to prostrate himself, and he didn't disappoint.

Haughty JD was unapologetic. "That's why Daddy's here, to help you eat dinner," he said, moseying up the length of the table.

Putting each of the kids back in their chairs, he pushed them in at their places, then kept going to seat himself at the head of the table, in pride of place.

Typical of JD to take the most eminent place in the room without invitation.

"Comfortable?" she asked, propping a hand on her hip.

JD tossed her a quick, impudent wink, then leaned toward the kids who were poking at their food again. "Is it good, buddy?"

"It was," Kye grumbled.

Sighing, if JD wanted the responsibility of getting them to eat, she wouldn't take it away from him.

"Kye spent so much time irritating his sister that I think it's almost cold," she said, returning to her chopping. "But they have to finish it."

"Can Daddy have some?" Sky asked.

Trust her children to take advantage of every situation. Whatever her daughter's ultimate goal, she'd guess it had something to do with a particular movie.

"You know how busy Daddy is," she said. "He doesn't want to eat dinner here. He probably has other places to be."

"Not tonight," he said. When she scowled at him, JD just bobbed his brows. "I'd love some pasta… thank you."

The food would still be warm. Going to the pot on the stove, she scooped a meager portion into a bowl and took it to him with a fork, dumping it onto the table.

"This is all quite domesticated, isn't it?" JD said, wearing a smile as he picked up the fork. "Civilized."

Oh, he was so proud of himself and loving every minute.

"It's novel for you," she said. "The rest of us call it life."

He popped a piece of pasta between his lips and surprised her by closing his eyes on a groan of bliss. "Oh my God, this is incredible," he said, forking up more to fill his mouth.

The pasta wasn't that good. She never worried about poisoning her kids, but her cooking skills weren't exactly of the highest order. The food she made was edible, though not as edible as their grandmother's, as she'd been told without subtlety. Four-year-olds were rarely subtle.

But he wasn't mocking her. It was a ploy. JD wasn't ignorant to the sway he had with their children. This was him using that influence for her benefit. Their twins idolized their father. Utterly idolized him. There was no other word for it. He could do no wrong.

So although she sighed at his melodramatic reaction to the meal, inside, she was grateful. Their beautiful babies were gazing at their father, eyes wide in wonder as he gobbled up the pasta like it was the most incredible thing he'd ever tasted.

She hid a smile.

"You two better hurry, or I'll be moving on to yours next," JD said, his mouth full.

So uncouth for a man known for his manners. It took all of her energy not to laugh when both kids suddenly copied their father's exuberance for the pasta. He glanced over his shoulder and winked at her again.

Okay, so that got a small smile, but she shook her head too. "Wow, look at you three go. I must be in the wrong trade," she said. "I should open my own five-star restaurant."

"Maybe you should," JD said.

He'd done what was needed; the kids were eating. He slowed until they weren't looking anymore and tried to rise from his chair.

THREE

THEIR DAUGHTER WAS faster than him.

Sky leaped to her knees on her seat and grabbed JD's wrist before he could stand up. "Daddy!"

Lowering back into his seat, the caught JD surrendered to his fate. "Yes, Sproutette?" he asked, opening his mouth to pop the ear Sky had attempted to deafen.

Their daughter was arranging her remaining pasta into a row, not letting any pieces touch, and then eating them in order. "Are mermaids good?"

"Are mermaids good?" JD asked and glanced at her for direction; she gave a discreet nod. "Uh, yes, Sproutette. Mermaids are excellent. I love mermaids."

Kye blew a raspberry.

"Kye," Rylee warned. "We don't mock each other's interests. Your sister doesn't make fun of your mural, does she?"

Each of the children had chosen murals for their bedroom walls based on things they loved.

"Mermaids are for girls," Kye said.

JD's head tilted. What was he thinking about? His children's reactions to each other or the seashell bikinis?

It was left to her to play parent. "If Daddy likes mermaids, that should be proof enough for you, son, that mermaids are not for girls. Daddy's not a girl, is he?" Perfect opportunity to have a little fun. "I tell you what, sweetpea," she said. "If everyone clears their plates, Daddy will watch all the *Little Mermaid* with you, Sky. How does that sound?"

Her daughter gasped, glittering with excitement. "Really, Daddy? In my bedroom? You'll watch the mermaids?"

JD took his turn to glare at her, but she just plastered a grin on her face. She always wished he'd spend more quality time with the kids and wouldn't snub the opportunity to encourage him.

"He'll watch the mermaids," she said and blinked at him with innocence. "You did say you were free tonight, right? And you want to embrace your daughter's passions."

"Maybe I could take Kye to the park, toss the ball around and—"

"It's too late for that," she said. "Kye will watch the movie with you."

Though her son would bluster and gripe, it wasn't such a hardship for the little guy. He sang the songs and quoted the dialogue just as well, if not better, than Sky. Whenever she noticed him singing along, she'd never point it out or make him self-conscious.

Seeing their children happy and enjoying themselves was the greatest pleasure for any parent. As it should be for JD too. He'd stood up to presidents, met monarchs, and been locked in merciless negotiations with some of the most ruthless executives. He'd face any of those situations and come out on top. Yet thinking about watching Disney with a four-year-old was making him tug at his collar.

Rinsing her hands, she dried them again and went to stand next to where he was sitting, facing him.

Propping her ass against the table, she bent over to loosen his tie. "The Great Mr. Jamison Dawes," she murmured. Sliding the tie free of his collar to toss it over her shoulder, she unfastened the top two buttons of his shirt. "Afraid of bedtime?"

"Me? Afraid? No, I'm not afraid. I do this all the time."

Had he forgotten how well she knew her children and their routines? All their routines, even those that didn't happen under her roof.

"Your mom doesn't let them watch movies at bedtime. Usually, I don't either, but since you're here, I'll allow you to rebel with them." She leaned forward to whisper. "I won't tell your momma, I promise."

Sky climbed off her chair, drawing the parents' attention from each other. Their little one reached up to take her empty plate from the table and went past them into the kitchen to put it into the dishwasher. Amazing.

"Can we have popcorn, Mommy?" she asked.

So much for their little bellies being full.

"Yes," she said, going to her daughter to crouch to her level and kiss her. "Sky, sweetpea, you're a good girl for putting your plate away. Are you trying to impress Daddy?"

"Daddy need to know the plate washer," Sky said, touching Rylee's hair. Her tresses always fascinated her daughter. "He didn't knowing."

"And Daddy will need to know where it is, so he can put his dirty bowl in the dishwasher, that's true. Good thinking, Sky," she said. Standing to smile at him, she ran a hand down their daughter's hair. "When was the last time Daddy did any kind of chore?"

JD didn't answer and probably didn't appreciate her smirk, though he didn't let it show. Funny how they kept locking eyes like this. It was quite a battle of wills to maintain their poker faces in front of their children.

"Grama makes him," Kye said.

Ha! She snorted a laugh. "Your mom?" she asked. "Your momma makes you do chores? Oh, and I thought I couldn't love that woman more."

"I'm housebroken, Ry," JD said, rising to take his empty bowl to the dishwasher.

She twirled a strand of Sky's hair around her finger. "I wouldn't know."

"No, you wouldn't," he said, meeting her body with his as she turned toward him, letting the little one's soft hair drift from her digit. Up close to JD, this was just an extension of the staring. Neither would break and back away. "I'm surprised, it's a turn on to hear you call me daddy. Where are we on that fetish these days?"

If he thought flirting or talking sex would rattle her, he'd misjudged his audience. "That's what you are to my babies," she stated. "That's why I call you it."

"You gave birth to my children," he said. "That's why it's a turn on."

Much as she'd love to push this to its limit just to triumph, and she would triumph, she chose to be critical instead.

"Said babies are in the room, JD. One day you should read a book about responsible parenting. You get them on audio now, so you don't have to tax yourself. Do you talk like this when your mom's around?"

He smiled. Sky's little fingers moved into her hand and JD's at the same time. Their daughter swung each parent's hand.

"What's a turn on?" Sky asked.

Her lips curled in triumphant satisfaction. "Daddy will explain it to you, sweetpea. Why don't you get the movie set up and Daddy will bring the popcorn?"

Sky kissed each of their hands and then spun around to run into her room.

"I'll explain it?"

"Just be happy she didn't pick up on 'fetish.' By the time you go through with the popcorn, she'll have forgotten about it. She will have a list of a thousand things to tell you in her room. Be careful what you say around them."

"Usually I'm worried about what I say in front of my mom, so I don't have to worry about them."

She retrieved the popcorn and put it in the microwave to cook. "She'll love showing you her room," she said. "The mural isn't fully painted, but the outline is there."

"They both have murals? If the guy's slacking, I'll call him and—"

She laughed and went over to bag the carrot sticks in individual portions. "I'm doing it myself," she said, taking the baggies across to the other side of the room.

"Momma, I don't want the carrots!" Kye whined when he saw her putting them in the fridge.

"I know, baby. Sky likes carrots. Mommy made apple snacks for you and you'll both have to share the grapes."

"I like the grapes."

"So does Sky," she said, going back toward the island. "You have to share. Besides, why are you whining about tomorrow's snack when you haven't even finished dinner? Sky's all done, and you're still at the table, young man."

"Daddy sat with Sky," Kye whimpered.

She prodded JD in the ribs. "Go sit with your boy."

"We have to talk about work," he murmured.

Stepping back, she met his eye, giving him a glare of disapproval. "That's why you came here? Work? Not to see your children?"

His eyes narrowed. "You're judging me."

"Always," she said and prodded him again. Judging? Yes. Surprised? No. JD was the way he was. That was that. Getting upset or starting a fight wouldn't change anything. JD got away with a lot with most people. Money did that. While she wouldn't necessarily start a war with him, she would never be one of those sycophants. If she was unhappy or questioning, she wouldn't hesitate to let him know. "Help Kye finish so he can watch the movie with you. Otherwise we'll be here all night."

"Will you be watching with us?"

Laughing, she moved the last of the daycare snacks to the fridge. "No, I have a ball-buster of a boss. I have work to do."

He propped himself on the counter beside her. "Want me to talk to him?"

She rearranged a few things in the fridge. "Ha! Yeah, right."

"Daddy!" Sky shouted from her room.

"We don't shout, Sky!" she called, closing the fridge to lean back and yell toward the mouth of the hallway beyond the end of the table. "Daddy is helping Kye with his food. They'll come to your room when he's done."

"I'm done," Kye said, pouncing out of his chair. "Let's go, Daddy."

"Uh, if your sister can do her plate, you can too. Come on," she said and went to take the popcorn from the microwave to put it in a bowl.

Kye put his plate away. "I pick the next one."

Smiling at their son, she bent to kiss his head. "Of course, little one," she said, straightening to take her amusement to JD, handing him the popcorn. "Enjoy, Daddy. Between the two of them, they have almost every animated movie ever released. You're in for a treat."

Kye took his daddy's hand to lead him toward Sky's room. JD looked back as though seeking escape, but he was only playing.

She'd known how her children felt about that man all their lives, while she'd spent most of that time judging him for his lack of involvement.

Her family had a routine. Her family and his. Why had JD suddenly decided he wanted to be a new cog in a machine that didn't need any spare parts? Their lives had been working just fine without him for years. Why was he choosing now to mix it up?

Read more from the Roxiverse in
Nothing to This...

Thank you for reading this tale!
If you can, please take the time to review.

~

Ask your local library for more Scarlett Finn
novels!

~

For all things Scarlett Finn
check out:

www.scarlettfinn.com

Next in the Roxiverse: